Once upon a time, long, long ago,
a bright star appeared in the sky.
It was there to tell the world about
the birth of a very important baby.
Everyone, from the humblest shepherd
to the wisest of wise men, wanted to
go and greet the newborn child.
Everyone, that is, except . . .

For Rose and Molly Syrett

Published in the United States 1998 by Dutton Children's Books,

a division of Penguin Putnam Books for Young Readers

375 Hudson Street, New York, New York 10014

http://www.penguinputnam.com/yreaders/index.htm

Originally published in Great Britain 1998 by Andersen Press Ltd, London

Typography by Alan Carr

Printed in Italy

First American Edition

ISBN 0-525-46079-9

2 4 6 8 10 9 7 5 3 1

The Shy Little Angel

RUTH BROWN

DUTTON CHILDREN'S BOOKS ❋ NEW YORK

"I'm not going!" said the little angel, stamping her foot. The other angels were shocked.

"You've got to go," they whispered. "Gabriel said that we *all* had to go. He said we had to shine like stars in the sky and then go down to greet the baby. Everyone will be there and you'll be in big trouble if you're not."

"Well, he won't know, will he?" said the little
angel. "If I stay up here and you don't tell him,
then he won't know."

"Yes, he will," chorused the other angels.
"Gabriel knows everything. He told us he did.
Don't you remember? He knows if you tell a lie. . . .

"He knows if you stick your tongue out at some-
one, and he always knows if you say a bad word,"
they all told her. "So he'll definitely notice if you're
not there. Come on!"

But the shy little angel would not go with them, and so they left her alone in the dark.

"I don't care," she muttered. "I don't want everybody staring at my halo and wings.

"Besides, I can see everything from up here."

The little angel looked down at the scene below. Although she didn't want to join in, she certainly didn't want to miss anything.

She saw the shepherds with their lambs.

She saw the three wise men carrying their precious gifts of gold, frankincense, and myrrh.

She saw the innkeeper and his wife, the cow, the horse, the donkey, and the angels.

She leaned forward just a little further to see them all gathered around, gazing in silent wonder at the tiny baby.

Suddenly the darkness just slipped away.

Everyone looked up. The little
angel was bathed in light from the
scene below.

The little angel didn't move. She was terrified.
But just as her lip began to tremble, the silence was
broken by the sound of loud applause echoing
around the auditorium.

The little angel, shining brighter than
the brightest star, smiled—

—and so did everyone else. Especially the
school principal, Mr. Gabriel.